AF583213

A story of desire and adventure...

...She dips her nose to his neck,
crosses the first barrier: ash,
the last cigar smoked.
She inhales deeper, his own musk—
the one he cannot wash off—releases.
She fills her lungs to capacity...

Praise for *Decoupled*

To read *Decoupled* is to link memory to mystery, to reach for stars that change their shape with every switch of railway track. We accompany a woman's journey by train through reminiscence as she links lovers to the fractured pieces of her former selves. "The train / of desire / starts down the tracks / collecting: lips, eyes, hips." Armstrong encourages readers to step off in order to immediately step on again, into another car, yearning for yet another beloved.
Kalehua Kim, author of *Mele* (Trio House Press)

Decoupled invites readers into a raw and sensorial exploration of an independent woman navigating desire. A woman deemed lost wanders the rails, experiencing various men along the way. Is she dreaming from the confines of her schoolhouse, or has she jumped aboard the newly-laid rail? Moving through the complexities of obsession, these poems navigate the emotional journey of longing for something beyond the self.
Laura Titzer, Author of *Omissions*

A narrative in verse, *Decoupled* unfolds the erotic life of The Woman as she travels through the West. Structured as a dramatic work, the collection employs potent Archetypes, each character offering The Woman a space to grapple with and enact desire. "The Dancer, The Astronomer, The Cartographer, and The Engineer / each contain a cargo of truth; / a flash of a story…the touch of each man's lips on her belly; / the taste and flavor of each man." These characters swirl around each other in continuous motion—the train, the dance, the stars, the breath. Under this motion quieter questions unfold, addressing the vulnerability of memory and of remembering: "she looks from man to man, from memory to memory, and leaves articles of herself with each." *Decoupled* skillfully grapples with questions of desire and mind, asking *Where can the erotic take you?* Come find out.
Rebecca Morton, author of *Clown* (Tupelo Press)

Tulipwood Books | Mercer Island, WA
tulipwood.org

Published 2026 by Tulipwood Books
Edited and Designed by Lynne Ellis

Cover Art: Composite image. Source images used under CC0.

- William Notman & Son, "Lower Kicking Horse Canon, Near Golden," 1889-1890, The J. Paul Getty Museum, Los Angeles, 84.XA.736.11.74
- John K. Hillers, [Western Landscape], 1871-1885, The J. Paul Getty Museum, Los Angeles, 85.XO.38.41
- William H. Bell, "Yellow Pine, (Pinus ponderosa, Doug.,) the timber-tree of the high pleateaus in Utah, Arizona, and New Mexico.," 1872, The J. Paul Getty Museum, Los Angeles, 84.XC.1144.37
- Frederick and William Langenheim, "Niagara Falls, Summer View, Suspension Bridge, and Falls in the Distance," about 1856, The J. Paul Getty Museum, Los Angeles, 2000.10.218
- People's Publishing Co., Map of Arizona, 1890, State of Arizona Research Library- Arizona State Library, G4330 1890

First Edition

ISBN: 979-8-9914048-6-0 (print-on-demand)

Library of Congress Control Number: 2026942512

Tulipwood Books is located on the unceded lands of the Duwamish, Muckleshoot, Cayuse, Umatilla, and Walla Walla people—past and present—who have cared for this land since time immemorial. These people are are still here, continuing to honor and bring light to this heritage, and we have great gratitude for their work. Find out more at native-land.ca and duwamishtribe.org

DECOUPLED

Erin
Armstrong

Tulipwood Books 2026

To Nate, thank you for secretly being a writer.

Poems

DECOUPLED

Our Characters

The Woman…lost

The Engineer…an inquirer

The Astronomer…a poet who hides his written work from the world

The Dancer…from an unknown place and time

The Cartographer…an accidental professional

The Musician…a stranger under a bridge

I

The Woman's Evening Train

arrives ten minutes late and at the edge of dusk.

The deciduous trees grasp at the remains of their leaves;
ponderosa pine preserve their bustle skirts in October twilight.

The Engineer stands on the platform preserved
in a time meant for lovers.

The train in the distance, two people stride arm in arm
toward the middle of town. The faint sound of the train's
whistle divides twilight from evening.

The scents of salted pork and roasted corn slip
in and out of buildings as they leave the town
of their imagination, entering
the reality of the city:

women laugh in saloons, pool balls click,
a fiddler speeds up his beat.

Dust settles between them as night dawns.
Neither of them brave enough to speak;
the truth walks invisible between them.

They continue toward the sounds of laughter
and the hoots of dancers. They see the oil lamps
begin to glow as partners clasp each other's hands
and slide back and forth to the music.

Years ago, they kissed bourbon and smoke lingered
on the tips of their tongues like a drink yet to be
created.

He carries her suitcase, a gentleman of the West,
one who is a different kind of wild.

In another story, one of them would lead
the other inside the hotel, demand a room
from the innkeeper, and they'd find themselves naked
on top of worn carpet.

Tonight, they avoid the possibility of the past.
He leads her home, nods his head goodnight,
leaves her standing in her husband's domain—
a strange yet familiar place.

She watches as he strides down the dirt path,
never turning back, evading any memories
that could be created in the present.
Each of his footsteps kicks up dust,
settling quickly, as if he was
never there at all.

The Bullet Train

carries five passengers—
who race through the station
at two hundred miles per hour—
passing by memories:

love as a routine line,
love as a wild chase
down the abandoned
track laid long ago.

So The Woman
gathers her passengers,
creates stories
between these
people who forget
the second
the story speaks.

Only she remembers
where she has gone,
who she's seen,
what she's tasted,
smelled, drawn,
touched, found.

The men
slip on and off
the track, unable to remember
anything but the station
where they began
and where she released
them from her car.

The Passengers

The Dancer, The Astronomer, The Cartographer, and The Engineer each contain a cargo of truth;
a flash of a story:

The men let The Woman on and off their cars until she satisfies her curiosity;
until she's traveled to all the places kept most secret—the smell of sweat around the base of the neck;
the touch of each man's lips on her belly;
the taste and flavor of each man.

The Dancer steps his quadrille in time with saloon girls.
The Astronomer looks to find Saturn's rings once more.
The Cartographer erases his imperfect maps.
The Engineer lays his new track in place of the broken one.

The Woman walks in and out of their cars—gathering her souvenirs:
a taste of whiskey to loosen her hips; maps of routes to travel;
the numbers of the fastest trains; Sirius or Canopus to light her way.

The Woman looks from man to man, from memory to memory, and leaves articles of herself with each man:
a book, a poem, a strand of hair, a fastener.
And on each man she drapes her scent,
linking each man's car to her train which
rides perpetually toward the station.

Map Makers

The Cartographer grabs The Woman's hand and twirls
her until she's pressed against his ship.
His hands clasp her lower back, her breath
quickens. It is easy to be naked yet clothed
as he drinks in her scent. She's the voyeur
to their embrace, the interpreter, the ignorant reader.
He removes the obstacles of her hair so his nose
can caress her skin; he transforms from map maker
to explorer, navigating the space between
her collarbone and her chin. He marks
each part of her flesh as new terrain, a place
to note, discover. Her untouched land
vibrates. She can feel his curiosity—
longing to understand the length of an aspen
branch or the smell of rain rising from the yellow
pine after the monsoon clouds assembled;
She can feel his maps divulging places—
the ones she wants locked away
from the explorers, the eccentrics, the orators of time.
She grasps for a blindfold, a way back to the darkness,
but her back arches under his palms.

A couple diverges like a river:

The Woman on one river bank;
The Cartographer on the other.

On her desk in the schoolhouse,
an apple decays;
fruit flies swarm to the roof.

Confessions in the night,
a blackness too dark;
no star glows.

On her side of the river,
The Woman sways to a quiet violin.
Naked in the rain; she hears no water fall.

She stifles her cry
as the wheels of the train
hit the tracks.

The Woman's love robbed
by an older man, one who
entered when the door was closed.

The Dancer

speaks words of wisdom
to The Woman lying on her bed
of chaos—
she can feel her head go up
and down in rhythm to his chest
as he whispers.

Moments of pleasure are not worth the pain.
Women are not meant to be understood but loved.
Men graying should not intertwine bodies
with women just ending their youth.

She hears each line, strokes the hair on his chest.
His music stops; she hears only their breath
out of sync.

Moonlight Alignments

The moon bursts orange as Earth eclipses the sun. The Astronomer and The Woman huddle together at the base of the San Francisco Peaks staring straight up into the orange-lit gray. Others from town move back and forth watching the different shades of light unveil. Nearby, a group of youthful girls chatter. They hear echoes of their observations as the moon glows; red wisps of light gather above their heads. They see fire. This eclipse marks the evening of their years together. The first time they kissed they looked at the stars: Orion, the Big Dipper, Polaris. The constellations were their friends while they were strangers to each other. The moon switches to a new shade of gray.

That Which Travels Down

Under the bridge of music
a man plays his saxophone,
echoing his beat off the surface
of the river, waiting for a stranger,
for an audience of now,
to hear his ephemeral song.
He holds the sad hollowness
of the moment on a tattered raft.
People float on the memories
of music, drifting toward his calling
but spiraling back and
forth with the ebb of the river,
so they never touch.

Under the shadow of his bridge,
he meets The Woman in the minutes
of his playing, but it is only in the reverberation
of his breath, which travels down
a track of the present;

she passes him under his bridge.
The echoes of his call grow
and her gaze meets his, locking
onto his cries; she does nothing
but look at his bare head and white shirt,
does nothing but wonder how
he has exposed her body,
as she touches her fingers
toward the sky and lets them dance.
Before she can do anything
more than smile the music
is replaced by shrieks of laughter
from her pupils, her classroom,
and the bridge of music vanishes.

The Woman

navigates
each track
with a star
a misstep, mapless;
she moves parallel
on her train
of desire
echoes ahead
never in sync
with the footprints
she makes
in the dust
twists and turns, spinning
unable to move
until a bell rings out reverberating around the station
white clouds burst from the smokestack

forward she must go

The Engineer,

oblivious, climbs rail
ties out of breath;
he wears a silver belt and worn boots.

Tonight, he peers over the bridge at the train
passing below and his mind floats away
toward The Woman he wants to forget.

These trains roll through his small towns
and he examines the ins and outs
of that which needs repairing, mending.

The Woman haunts:

buttons travel the length of her skirt,
the cinch of her belt accentuates her waist
while the lace of her neck points to her delicate chin.

These fragments he pushes into the farthest
crevices of his memory—
hiding pictures he wills to fade.

Yet the night comes and
the images return—like the trains
coming and going on his tracks.

We sleep and when we wake, we unfold

As sleep breaks, the weight of memories
from the night calls back

There we lay head to head
drawing maps of the evening;
the curves of our backs   canyons;
the sharpness of our elbows   boulders.
In between these rocky ledges,
from breast to hip bone a trail
from belly to elbow a waterfall
the way our hair entangled foliage.

In the night we lose ourselves hiking
through these unknowns; we ascend
toward the trails we hear calling.

We look for the highest mountain to rest
our weary bodies and sleep when ascension's
achieved. We dance in our minds
until the music dies with the first hint of day.
We sleep and when we wake, we unfold
our accordion selves, smooth out the creases
and crinkles so we can retrace, redraw
our bodies once more.

The Woman dreamwalks on an unkempt trail

where her lover cannot
find her.
A marbled green eye
peels her back limb by limb.
A shame sits
below her belly;
she waits, for a quick
relief to ease
the disequilibrium
settling over her eyes, her nose,
her mouth. Yearning for
a sleep so peaceful
she will not remember
to wake. The mist
of a waterfall will
linger off the river
and shroud her
from the stare she fears.

The Astronomer

distracts her
through Saturn's rings,
Vega's brightness in Lyra,
the orange dance of Mars.

He takes her through space
with his concave mirrors,
lines their way forward,
the infinite possibilities
surround each particle,
each piece of the universal
puzzle.

When she feels most on edge,
he tightens his grip, inhales
the smell from her hair and neck,
so she leans back as he propels
them toward Earth.

While they spin, she feels
safe in the dark.

Circling the Dancer's Dreams

Under the outstretched hand of Saint Anne,
she wonders how you lie in your time,
in your place, are you still examining
the night stars that twinkle or watching
the planets stand still in their orbit?
As she goes through time, in your future,
she stumbles over cobblestone, glancing
at the men: sun-kissed skin stretches across
their faces, yet they take no notice of hers;
unafraid of beautiful women they gaze
without worry, without care, and the stares
they release bore into the backs of the women
who stride up and down the streets, so she
remembers you, the patient lover, the one
who held a kindness so strong any fear
vanished and she circled your dreams.

The Woman

alone in her teacherage:
free to dress in silence,
take her breakfast;
walk the mile to the schoolhouse;
wait for girls to line up on one side,
boys on the other; wait
to file onto the dusty wood floors,
hang coats, put lunch pails on the shelf;

she'll stand at the front, as she does every day;
ensure they've made their manners:
a curtsy, a bow before reading begins.

Here, she feeds her mind
and wanders like her charges
to the stars or onto maps
she draws in her head;
she imagines where Saint Christopher
would take her as pupils recite,

read, wrestle with a letter or number;
she hears the rumblings of construction,
a clanging of wood onto metal tracks;
she knows the schoolhouse as her home;
as her mind travels outside on the trains
being built.

Out at sea, The Woman searches

for a map—
the one which belongs to the elusive
Cartographer.

She feels sick
as the waves drown
her ship; her boat
never meant for these waters.

She hears the voices
of those who once loved
a lost hero; they sing
of a wandering
ghost.

As she voyages,
she hears The Astronomer
pointing to the Pleiades
and The Dancer

echoing spells charming
her off course.

Her memories of The Engineer
keep her ship afloat,
while she wanders the sea
searching for a man of maps.

He has seen the peaks
of high mountains, swum
in deep lakes, touched
collections of lands, tongued their waters
and heard their songs.

She searches for The Cartographer;
the one who waits
to be found.

The train

of desire
starts down the tracks
collecting: lips, eyes, hips.
On one platform waits
a single passenger,
sun-drenched in a starched white dress;
straw hat fastened to brunette curls;
the boots of her black heels keeping time
to a music only she can hear.
The conductor waves her aboard.
The Woman ascends the steps,
grabs her skirts, sees the future.
As the train lurches forward,
she sees, from the vestibule,
a mirage of her past.

II

II

The Terrors of My Love For You

You've annihilated the land given, buried your scorched earth. Above,
    a prairie breathes yellow grass
and whips in the wind. The forest of ponderosa stretches beyond
    where I am allowed, vast and empty; you watch, a specter
    haunting the places you've burned.

The wind switches direction and I smell fire. I know these places.

They are perpetually inflamed.

They are the circles of rings you have sown. The ones that could not

be stamped out. These are the embers

scattered across the forest floor.

At the entrance of this land stands an archway of rock. This is where I lie.

From here, the land mines whisper and call. They are hidden so deep no one should travel this trail. From my rock, I see what was, is, and will be.

I see your past—she waves at me in a white gown, holds the hand of another, a woman dressed in azure. I see another—unaware, she lifts her red dress to her knees and calls back to him, her voice echoing off the ridges of the wind. The last woman I see—the embittered future who stands with her head cloaked in black. She bows toward the ground but does not weep. These women, flags of danger, poppies urging me to sleep. I should come no farther through the already-burnt earth.

From my cushion of rock, I wave to my celestial companion. The one whose permission I sought and was granted. He stands with the reflection of tears behind his eyes.

*
**

Let me burn, I say.

■

III

III

Hide the Map Not Yet Drawn

put the unfinished
map of her body away.

Let the black charcoal
lines fade into an ashy dust
but remain visible

for the day when you pull
it out and venture
beyond her collarbone,
beyond the flesh between
the crux of her elbow and forearm,
beyond where her hips
reside.

Or if you cannot wait,
draw an invisible map
of the places you desire
to find, to inhale

so that you cannot inhabit
the place without thinking
of her arches, curves, and contours.

The Woman you want
to draw.

The Woman you want
to remember, to revisit,
to suck

until she cries out
like the lighthouse
spinning its lights.

Switch Track:

last evening's delight
shatters with a sound of a woodpecker
burrowing its beak in the aspen.

On repeat, she sees places
where their bodies touched: lips pressed,
hands circled around hips, caressed
backs, and stroked hair.

She dresses for a day with pupils.
Laced boots, knots in a tie,
her skirt pressed.
The images flip
from moment to memory.

The Woman As Passenger

Here she is

the halter

in the ephemeral

of yesterday

her hips this ass to slap

after she is gone

you will jettison
her clothes to the floor

The Woman lying in your bed

who could read your maps

to the sky above

The Woman

of time

she becomes the now

the woman you taste

yearn for her

on a rainy Sunday morning

deep with secrets

in the present

others slip away

to a celestial ether

you want

a scent that remains

on crocheted blankets

not yet created

a woman

who would announce

she is not that woman.

The Woman

takes The Cartographer
behind the depot;
a train stands like a witness.
She leads the expedition,
traveling like a curious virgin,
clawing through the fear
of being in his arms once more.
She dips her nose to his neck,
crosses the first barrier: ash,
the last cigar smoked.
She inhales deeper, his own musk—
the one he cannot wash off—releases.
She fills her lungs to capacity.
His hands are cuffs surrounding her hips.
He burrows his face close to her neck,
and she can do nothing but pant
as the tip of his nose strokes each vein.

Observatory Time

The Astronomer drifts
on scraps of time

pausing
floating

toward her

He presses
palm to palm

They shapeshift
into bodies
of their past
they forget

how to morph
into their future

so they remain
stuck in their capsule
of now

their bodies fade

inside
the train car

oil lamps rattle on
wicker tables

they forget

to remember

how they came together

She's Gone Roaming the Rail Beside the Ponderosa Pines

He wakes to find The Woman gone;
he did not hear the goodbye
said in the darkest of the night.

He wakes to count
the tedium of minutes,
hours in her time.

He wakes to find
a mountain echoing
the calls of Saint Teresa.

He wakes to remember
the length of her tresses
the bluest of her eyes.

He wakes to hear the sorrow
of ending and confuses
it with his dreams.

He wakes to the laughter
of children and they drown out
the rhythm of her voice.

He wakes to find the ghost
of The Woman gone
in the last seconds of sleep.

Think not of The Woman

in red pumps and a black dress who
you saw once on the platform
across from yours.

Wonder not where she went or who
she saw but rather how she moved
in her patent shoes that shined sunlight.

Think of her ankles crossing
as she took her seat and raced
toward a destination of encounters:
men who offered her scotch and swung
her high above their heads until
she whooped in delight.

Think of her harnessing her black
valise on the platform and wonder
how many letters she may have written
of her love for you.

Take your maps from your travels
and think of The Woman who once
stood before you on a platform
of unrequited love.

The Holler of a Red-Tailed Hawk

The end comes in a slow dissolve.
Neither party realizes they divided
themselves into two different people
who can no longer unite.

Other loves are imagined yet
let go while the two stare
across the railroad tracks unsure
who crossed first.

The Engineer trickles into the distance;
he slips onto the backside of mountain slopes;
he cannot be found nor heard
as he whispers his goodbye.
The Woman is silent to his last call.

The letters cease to exist.
There is no sound; the forest
is empty save for the hawk
whose harsh cry marks the end.

The next train arrives;
The Woman stumbles into the car
toward a destination of solitude.

Sheild a Woman's Secrets

Write declarations of love to an imagined man.
Read a map upside-down.

Argue for hours about the rail's destruction.
Hear ravens screech on rooftops.

Take an oversized shirt off a bare body.
Peel a carrot down to its flesh.

Wander through the tracks of impulse.
Jam a dozen roses into a crystal vase too small.

Deny the mistakes you have made.
Bury the voices in the sounds of wheels screeching.

Write a poem for the men that do not exist.
Shield a woman's secrets inside a train car.

Decoupled

we undo

what we already
began the brief tingle
of hair against a cheek
the stroke of a hand
on the small of the back

we will

unwind

the moments

we remember

in the arms
of another

we forget

deconstruct

the earth crumbled

we remember
a rigid track of memory

side by side

on our train forward
we begin

joined without a jolt

Tell me

why you came for me.
why do you haunt my halls,
devoid and empty of time?
What were you hoping to find
between the bridges of my lips,
between the wedges of my toes?
What can I give to you?

Now that we are here, how
shall we move together?
Will we dance hand in hand,
bounding down a sidewalk
of fear? Or shall it be a march,
single file where neither of us knows
the steps of the other? We could float
like strangers down a calm river,
not giving each other a nod,
a glance, or a subtle smile.

Tell me why you are here,
for you know I already
disappeared.
Tell me of all your fantastical desires,
for you know I will vanish into ash.
Tell me why you came for me,
so I can become the embers
dying in your mouth.

Parallel to the rail cars, The Woman floats

on a starry night. Love of different
kinds fades to black without feeling or flight.

Their love was not crossed but entangled.
Her star reflects no light down to Earth,
for not a soul knows of her existence.
The death of light fades, becoming
a moment of static in the ephemeral,
a love lost, the moment remembered.

In the purple night sky,
the memory of ghosts meander
an unnavigable road—winding
to an edge where a scream
of pain sounds no different
than dynamite digging into a mountainside.
No different than the coyote cubs howling
for their lost mother.

Here the ghosts choose
the terror of their voices,
and remind the world of a pain
unimaginable until now.
A sound pierces the soul
of The Woman who understands
the cries of former lovers.

Among the box of maps,
The Cartographer keeps her
for a time when she can walk
the tracks beside the trains,
hear them hum as steam covers her.
She moves forward until
the white clouds evaporate
around her. In the distance a
final car slick with black lacquer
disappears.

God's Courtyard: the cobblestone corner

The woman says goodbye to her lover
outside the brick church. (he floats)
Morning light breaks.
He wanders God's courtyard,
(passing Saint Elizabeth's outstretched hand)
ignoring the Saint's wisdom.
Dust glides over God's mountains
and settles on the wooden steeples.
She watches the ground encircle her
(she remembers): she met him at the foot of Mary.
There she stood, and he draped his desire
over her in a language she could not understand.
Between their moments of pleasure,
(when the intimacy of silence struck)
secrets slipped between their lips.
(The love of others haunted their bed)
The thrust of his tongue to hers
allowed her to taste what might have
been: the begging in the night,

the cheeks to chest. When the first
rays of sun cast through their window,
they took each other's hands and walked
toward their obligations over the blush sand
which held the secret of their feet (like
the wall he pressed her against held
the last of their bodies), so she left a mark
so purple and blue that when he
wakes from the mist (he will find)
her teeth, her lips, the lick of her tongue.

The Ease of Imagining

the Southern drawl slow, like a train soothing
a passenger back and forth—he builds as he speaks—

wood planks go side by side until a story takes shape:

she does not know if she will hear his voice again;
she weaves her slate black hair through his present.

She waits for him on a mountain where snow melts
sees the soot from day's work and tastes it;

removes the suspender straps so she can reach to pull his shirt
and touch the muscles built from a lifetime of work

Dressed in blue silk, she sways—dancing a song only he can hear.
Her voice high until bits of wood burst around them.

Unmoored he presses his lips to hers finding a way back home,
until the climax of the story where they can remain invisible.

Under the Stars of the High Desert

The Woman searches for acceptance
buried in a chest of silk.

Her desire for The Astronomer flares
when he talks in circles of celestial curves.

She hears the chirps of mountain chickadees
lost in the darkest of the night.

The backup light flickers out;
the brake numbers disappear.

She silences him with a kiss.

Flying Junction

The Cartographer sings her a song
so deep it makes a crow's cry sound sweet.

He lifts her hips to his as the coyotes howl
near the forest's edge. She sees

patches of pine burned, the forest floor bare.
She's the investigator of space and destinations.

Maps of tracks already laid, routes drawn,
whip into the wind as she cries out with pleasure.

The Space Between

The Woman forgets the strip club turned steeple turned coffee shop;
the desert turned ocean turned evergreen; the creosote dirt turned
cherry blossoms; the man turned engineer turned mapmaker turned
stargazer, The Woman turned poet turned lover turned mother,
the girl turned curious,
turned woman, turned frenzied,
turned upside down.

She forgets the space between memory and living.

She forgets the train able to leave
and return without rearrangement
without order.

Awake in the Darkness of the Sleeping Car

The Woman finds herself stroking the glass windows,
hoping to touch the sea waving to her outside.
While the city lights twinkle, she remembers
her lovers not as fiction but as truth,
as promises made to endure the broken track,
to find the train lines most suited for the voyage.

She need not climb aboard trains of decisions
for she wanders, meanders
with her hands outstretched,
she is a gazer of humanity, a traveler of time
through place and memories built during a lifetime
together.

She weaves in and out of each car,
finding those destinations of seclusion
bearable in solidarity, in the silent
company of each other.
The others slip away,

climbing aboard the appropriate
platforms to find their own tracks,
their passengers of adventure.

For now, aboard her train of desire
she remains in her midnight travels.

The Woman tucks away the memories
in her valise above. She learns to forget,
to take the memories and examine
them when the windows darken
and the scenery goes quiet.

About the Author

Erin Armstrong's (she/her) work has appeared in several literary magazines, including *Mom Egg Review*, *seedfall*, *Anodyne Magazine*, *Indy Correspondent*, *Fiction Southeast*, *Black Heart Magazine*, *Lost Magazine*, *The Museum of Americana: a literary review*, and more. She received her MFA from the University of Arizona. She lives in Shoreline, Washington. More of her work can be found at www.erinarmstrong.org

Historical Note

Much of this story takes place during the expansion of the railroad in the western United States, particularly in Flagstaff, Arizona. While not mentioned directly in the book, the author would like to point out that—while the railroad brought a great deal of industrialized innovation and expansion for what would eventually become the modern United States as we now know it—the railroad and western expansion did lasting harm to those who already lived in the area. Indigenous people were forced to leave their homes, had violence inflicted upon them, and were aggressively mistreated by colonizers of white European descent. Because of these horrific acts, Indigenous people and cultures have suffered through years of generational trauma and systemic racism. Yet, they are still here. The author wants to encourage readers to learn more about the tribal nations of the area where this story takes place, and to become aware of the systemic harm that westward expansion caused. To this day, over 30,000 square miles of tribal lands around Flagstaff are home to the Havasupai, Hopi, Hualapai, Kaibab-Paiute, and Navajo peoples. To learn more about the history of Indigenous people in the area, please visit The Museum of Northern Arizona's *Native Peoples of the Colorado Plateau* exhibit and website, and engage with Flagstaff's local American Indian communities.

Acknowledgements

To my writing community, far and wide, I'm forever grateful for your support and your dedication to the craft of writing. For my group in Seattle, Lynne Ellis, Laura Titzer, Kalehua Kim, and Rebecca Morton (by way of Chicago), you all have pushed me outside of my comfort zone more times than I can count and lifted my poetry spirit over and over again. Thank you!

Even though it's been fifteen years, my Arizona writer friends and teachers have voices that are forever in my head and push me to be a better writer to this day. Thank you to Tim Dyke, Joel Smith, Glenn Grunberger, Kindall Gray, Beth Alvarado, Jason Brown, Manuel Muñoz, and Laynie Browne. Thank you to the University of Arizona Poetry Center where this all started. To Aurelie Sheehan, I'm sorry you won't ever read this, but please know you were part of the inspiration and the motivation to continue writing.

This book went through a strange and uphill path to publication, so thank you to all my friends who read drafts when I was ready to abandon the project entirely: Shannon Triplet, Shloka Mangharam, Travis Wood, Tim Dyke, Carol Lee, and Nate Stock. If you hadn't killed the negative voices in my head, I may have stopped writing this altogether!

Thank you to the following editors for publishing previous versions of these poems: "The Woman's Evening Train," "Hide the Map Not Yet Drawn," and "Wild West Nostalgia" were originally published by *Indy Correspondent*. "Map Makers," originally titled "The Cartographer," was published by *The Poet's Billow*. The original inspiration for this book came from a flash fiction piece I wrote called "Destination of Solitude" that was originally published in *The Museum of Americana: A Literary Review.*

Thanks to the help of Poets on the Coast and Hugo House. The teaching, mentorship, and writing prompts were invaluable and pushed me to continue to grow as a writer and reader.

Thank you to Lynne Ellis for going out on her own and starting a fabulous press, and then asking me to be a part of it. Creating art is no easy feat, and neither is helping get it into people's consciousness.

To all my friends, please know I started a long list in which each one of you was named, and in the end, there are just too many of you to be able to fit onto this page. Please know you have my deepest gratitude for all the support you provide me each day. Thank you for giving me space in your life.

To my family who, even if I am in a terrible mood or ignoring them by reading, will always show up: Alix Armstrong, Julia Armstrong, and Neal Armstrong.

To my girls, I love you so much. I'm so grateful that you all have allowed me the space to continue writing. When you grow up and start reading my work, I hope it isn't as strange as I expect it may be to see your mother on the page. I recommend picking up your own pen and paper and just writing about it.

Nate, you're my rock, my best friend, and partner. Thank you for everything you do every day to make our family and our relationship such a success. I love you.

A note on the typography

Decoupled is set in Centruy Old Style, designed by Morris Fuller Benton between 1908 and 1909. This typeface was a redesign of Century Roman—first cut by Linn Boyd Benton at American Type Founders in 1894, for use in *Century Magazine*. The poem titles in this book appear in LTC Globe Gothic, based on Taylor Gothic (also reimagined by Morris Fuller Benton in the early 1900s). Running heads are set in Della Respira, a digital typeface designed by Nathan Willis, based on Della Robbia (cut by ATF in 1913). The ornaments are a mix of Bodoni (Morris Fuller Benton once again, with his 1911 version of Giambattista Bodoni's 1790 design), Condor (David Jonathan Ross at DJR), and Graveur (Juanjo Lopez at MTM in Madrid, Spain).

More from Erin Armstrong...

My Orchid

I wander through
an aisle of purple orchids;
they bend toward me
until I stop
at my orchid—
wilting and dry and left
only with green leaves
shooting from its bottom.
I have no memory
of when it last bloomed—
four years ago perhaps
when my daughter arrived
it shed its last flower sometime
after my third pregnancy loss.
It kept its green leaves
but the branches that held flowers
turned brittle and beige.

I still tend it with ice cubes,
squeeze plant food into it.
I even tried replanting it once.
As it sits half-dead in my kitchen
windowsill, I wonder if it will
spend its life as a half-lived
flower or one day, when I'm
not looking, will a bud pop
up and start to grow.

www.ingramcontent.com/pod-product-compliance
Lightning Source LLC
LaVergne TN
LVHW031315160826
845673LV00013B/3013

* 9 7 9 8 9 9 1 4 0 4 8 6 0 *